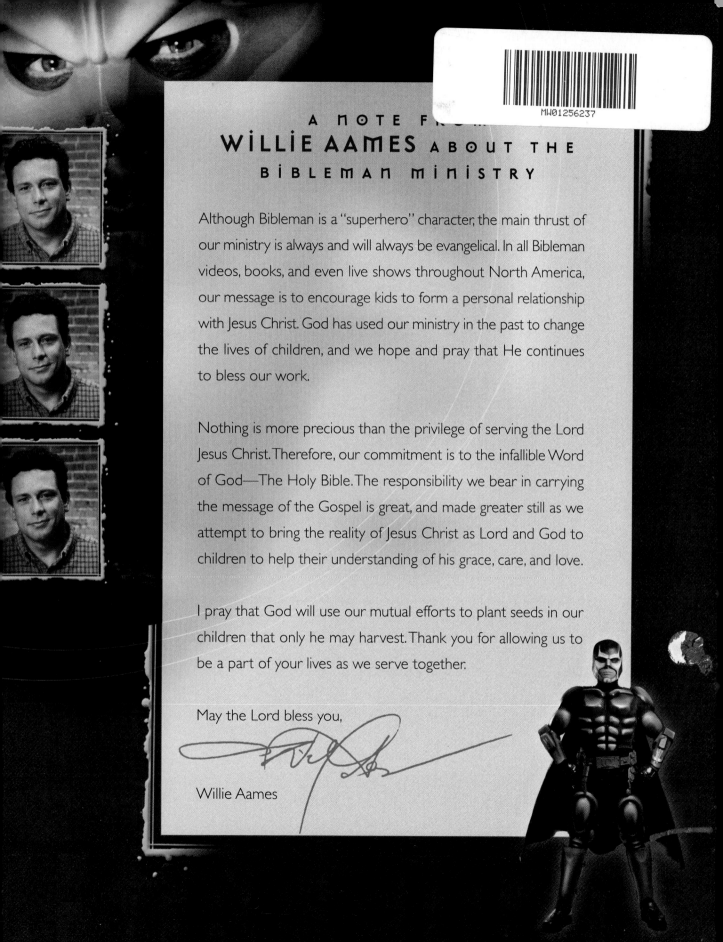

A NOTE FROM WILLIE AAMES ABOUT THE BIBLEMAN MINISTRY

Although Bibleman is a "superhero" character, the main thrust of our ministry is always and will always be evangelical. In all Bibleman videos, books, and even live shows throughout North America, our message is to encourage kids to form a personal relationship with Jesus Christ. God has used our ministry in the past to change the lives of children, and we hope and pray that He continues to bless our work.

Nothing is more precious than the privilege of serving the Lord Jesus Christ. Therefore, our commitment is to the infallible Word of God—The Holy Bible. The responsibility we bear in carrying the message of the Gospel is great, and made greater still as we attempt to bring the reality of Jesus Christ as Lord and God to children to help their understanding of his grace, care, and love.

I pray that God will use our mutual efforts to plant seeds in our children that only he may harvest. Thank you for allowing us to be a part of your lives as we serve together.

May the Lord bless you,

Willie Aames

Visit us on the Web at tommynelson.com

STAY TUNED TO THIS BibleChannel FOR EXCITING NEWS ABOUT
BiBLEMAN® ACTION FIGURES CURRENTLY UNDER CONSTRUCTION!

Bibleman® is a registered trademark of Pamplin Entertainment Corporation.

Published in Nashville, Tennessee,
by Tommy Nelson™, a division of Thomas Nelson, Inc.

Design: Lookout Design Group, Inc.

ISBN 0-8499-7574-3

Printed in the United States of America
01 02 03 04 05 PHX 10 9 8 7 6 5 4 3 2

PHiLLiPiANS 4:13 SAYS,

"i CAN DO **ALL**

THiNGS THROUGH

CHRiST

BECAUSE HE GiVES ME

STRENGTH."

I'M JUST A NORMAL GUY WITH PROBLEMS LIKE EVERYONE ELSE.
CONFIDENTIAL
U.N.I.C.E. REPORT
NAME: MILES PETERSON
NOT-SO-SECRET IDENTITY: BIBLEMAN
RESIDENCE: EAGLEGATE MANOR
BEST FRIEND: CYPHER
FAVORITE COLOR: PURPLE

BOTH MILES PETERSON AND

BIBLEMAN

ARE PLAYED BY ACTOR

WILLIE AAMES,

THE CENTRAL FIGURE

ON THE BIBLEMAN TEAM

SINCE 1995.

MILES PETERSON came from a family of wealth and became a very successful man in his own right. He had status, money, influence, everything he thought a person could want—except peace. This lack of peace eventually drove him into loneliness, sin, and pain— almost ruining his life. Then one day, he discovered God's Word and its power. Miles became a follower of and believer in Jesus Christ. And from that day forward, his life has been transformed. Now showing kids everywhere how to become stronger and defeat the forces of evil with the Word of God . . . he is BIBLEMAN!

PUT ON THE FULL
ARMOR OF GOD!

WAISTBELT OF
TRUTH

BREASTPLATE OF
RIGHTEOUSNESS

SHIELD O
FAITH

SWORD:

I carry the sword of the spirit which is energized in two ways: by the Word of God and my personal relationship with Jesus Christ. Although the power of the sword of the spirit is unlimited, its complete capabilities are unknown.

—BIBLEMAN

GRAPPLING HOOK:

U.N.I.C.E.

BIBLEMAN'S GRAPPLING HOOK HAS A 575-POUND CAPACITY, MICRO-BRAIDED WIRE THAT ENABLES HIM TO LAUNCH UP TO 80 FEET. BIBLEMAN CONCEALS HIS GRAPPLING HOOK WITHIN A SECRET COMPARTMENT IN HIS LEFT GAUNTLET.

GAUNTLETS:
(THE ARM PART OF HIS GLOVES)

Bibleman gets an additional boost from a pair of 500-feet-per-second mini-smoke rockets, which are both laser guided and heat seeking. These rockets are used for evasive maneuvers and concealment. They are located within the right gauntlet. His right gauntlet also contains a spring-loaded, power-sensor handle which scans refraction particle frequencies and the energy created by Bibleman's heart. This device enables lab operators U.N.I.C.E. and Cypher to monitor energy emitted from Bibleman's emotions and his sword of the spirit.

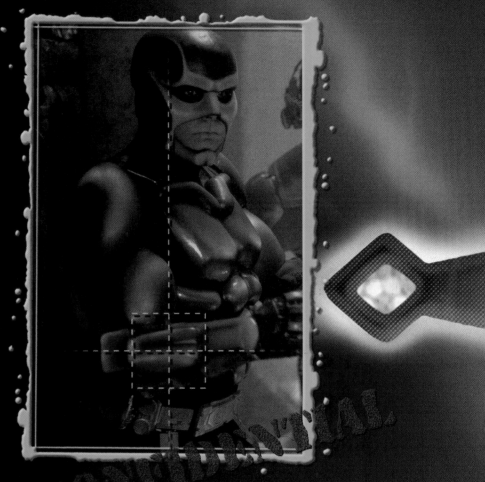

Bibleman does not get any power from his seal or his weapons.

His power comes from the Holy Spirit and his relationship with Jesus.
—WILLIE

BIBLEMAN'S SEAL:

CROSS : a representation of Christ

BIBLE : the unerring Word of God

FLASH : a symbol of the Son's light

CYPHER
(FAiTHFUL SiDEKiCK)

Cypher has always been a believer. Over the last few years, he has secretly been watching Bibleman and praying he would be called to join him in his quest to overcome evil. Bibleman's first sidekick was Coats, and once he was called to serve in an unknown destination, he passed the torch on to Cypher.

CONFIDENTIAL

U.N.I.C.E. REPORT

NAME: Cypher

RESIDENCE: Eaglegate Manor

BEST FRIEND: Miles Peterson

FAVORITE COLOR: Black

SPECTROSCOPIC HEADGEAR

Cypher's headgear features micro-processing chip lenses, which upload into a fiber optic prism. This prism breaks down light particles to their most basic form, thus enabling Cypher's vision of things not normally seen by the mortal eye. His job is to manage the laboratory's communications systems and assist Bibleman, providing tactical and technical support.

WHAT TOOK YOU SO LONG?

I WAS IN THE LITTLE SUPERHEROES' ROOM.

AND NOW A WORD FROM OUR SPONSOR:

NEHEMIAH 8:10B SAYS,

"THE JOY OF THE LORD WILL MAKE YOU STRONG."

BRADY WILLIAMS

JOINED THE

BIBLEMAN

TEAM IN 1999,
AND HE PLAYS THE ROLE
OF SIDEKICK CYPHER.

The Bible says in Proverbs 27:17 that as iron sharpens iron, so one person sharpens another. In this same way, Cypher and Bibleman encourage each other in their work to serve God and defeat evil.

> MILES CARES ABOUT PEOPLE AND IS ALWAYS WILLING TO DROP WHAT HE IS DOING TO HELP THEM OUT.
> — CYPHER

WHEN WE
ARE IN THE LAB,
MILES ALWAYS
SPILLS CHEMICALS
AND LOSES THINGS.
— CYPHER

I asked Willie if I could be Bibleman, but this was the only spot open. I guess I should just be thankful that I don't have to wear tights!
— BRADY

CYPHER
ABOUT
HIMSELF AND
HIS FAITH

I'm learning to rely on the power from the Word of God to fight the enemy. But I'm still new at this, so sometimes I forget and depend on my own strength—which never works.

— CYPHER

CYPHER:
ABOUT HIS FRIENDSHIP WITH

Bibleman is my best friend. His strength comes from knowing God, his Word, and how to apply that Scripture to real-life situations. Anyone can have that power. Just like all of us though, Bibleman is human. At times, he needs to be encouraged and reminded of the truths in God's Word—just as we all do.

— CYPHER

OUR ONLY CONCERN SHOULD BE DOING GOD'S WILL. VIOLENCE IS NEVER FUN!

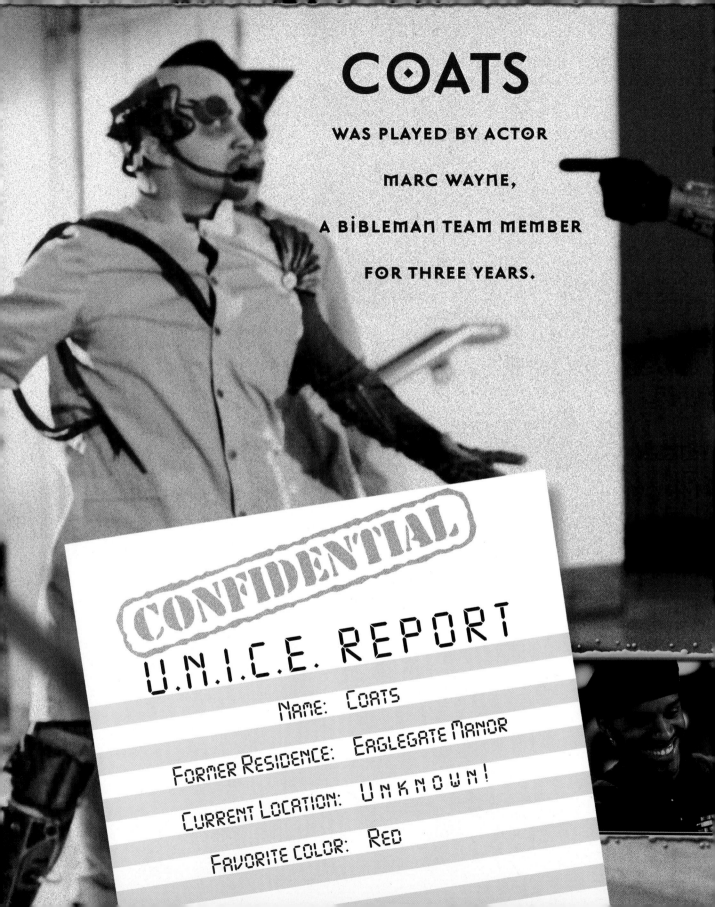

COATS

WAS PLAYED BY ACTOR

MARC WAYNE,

A BIBLEMAN TEAM MEMBER

FOR THREE YEARS.

CONFIDENTIAL

U.N.I.C.E. REPORT

NAME: COATS

FORMER RESIDENCE: EAGLEGATE MANOR

CURRENT LOCATION: UNKNOWN!

FAVORITE COLOR: RED

A CHILDHOOD FRIEND OF MILES PETERSON, COATS WAS BIBLEMAN'S TRUSTED FRIEND AND COHORT IN MANY ADVENTURES.

LOCATED IN SCHATZVILLE, USA,

EAGLEGATE MANOR

is home to Miles, Cypher, and U.N.I.C.E. Built in the twentieth century by Miles's great-grandfather, the house passed down through each generation. This classic stone manor is complete with secret passages and a sliding bookcase that reveals the entrance to Miles's laboratory. Hidden deep within the mansion's catacombs, Miles's lab is a place of prayer, refuge, study, and discovery.

EAGLEGATE MANOR

BACKSTORY:

A deep source of emotion for Miles, the mysterious circumstances surrounding the Peterson legacy have never been fully discussed or disclosed. It is possible that whatever his past contains compels Miles to shield his family history and drives him forward as

BIBLEMAN.

LABORATORY CAVE

U.N.I.C.E. REPORT

Facility: Laboratory

Location: Eaglegate Manor Catacombs

Monitor: U.N.I.C.E.

Capabilites: Can detect and transmit any signal including electronic and spiritual broadcasts

Security Systems: Heat-triggered movement and sound sensors, and a really big deadbolt!

BIBLEMAN

ABOUT THE LABORATORY CAVE

Of course, we get to the lab through secret, narrow passageways in Eaglegate Manor. But we also get in and out of the cave using a special tunnel for vehicles. The only people who have access to the cave are me, Cypher, and an occasional villain. U.N.I.C.E. actually lives in the lab, monitoring systems and keeping watch twenty-four hours a day.

—BIBLEMAN

Communication systems in the laboratory use the most advanced satellite systems, fiber optics, and thermal and super-cooled micro-ceramic technologies. This sophisticated system is capable of intercepting and transmitting any type of signal, including those broadcast on a spiritual level. This requires a tremendous source of energy, which is shielded by sound vibration and sixteen inches of lead surrounded by water-filled plexi-membrane.

YOU'D NEVER KNOW THIS PLACE USED TO BE A JACUZZI.

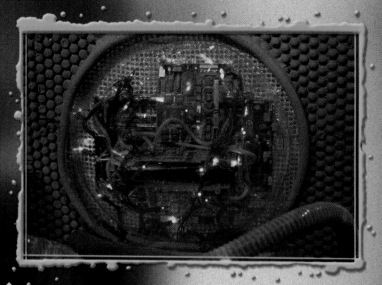

U.N.I.C.E.

UNIVERSAL NETWORKING
INTELLIGENCE COMPUTING ENTITY

CONFIDENTIAL

U.N.I.C.E. REPORT

NAME: U.N.I.C.E.

LOCATION: MILES'S LABORATORY

FUNCTION: DEFEATING EVIL

PROGRAMMER: CLASSIFIED!

CAPABILITES: FULL ACCESS TO VILLAIN'S
COMPUTER SYSTEMS

GLOBAL ACCESS: UNLIMITED SATELLITE AND
REMOTE OPERATIONS

THE U.n.i.C.E. (pronounced YOU-niss) mainframe consists of super-conductor CO_2 fiber optics, as well as the calculating intelligence of 16 MPAR 3 giga computers. She can assimilate and access over 100 trillion bytes of information per second. Bottom line: U.N.I.C.E. is the fastest, smartest computer ever made. Easily updated, U.N.I.C.E. contains a personality chip that allows her to maintain her own identity. She is voice-activated and can scan frequencies of any person entering the room to immediately identify their ability to access laboratory databases. She is capable of molecular, sub-molecular, and sub-atomic scanning through laser technologies, which are not yet available to the outside world.

TOP SECRET

The Falcon does not use gasoline, but its classified energy source may not be revealed in print. Falcon scans surrounding topography and adjusts its terrain profile to meet its rider's needs. With an optional sidecar kit, the motorcycle is fully shielded, using stealth technology. Falcon has night vision equipment and is heat resistant. Equipped with titanium alloy wheels, direct drive, a CD player, and full communications systems, Falcon has an exceptionally cool "AOOGAH" horn.

FALCON
BIBLEMAN'S MOTORCYCLE

CONFIDENTIAL

U.N.I.C.E. REPORT

Name: Falcon

Energy Source: Classified

Residence: Eaglegate Manor

Capabilities: Stealth, Night Vision, Heat Resistance

Optional: Sidecar Kit

Batteries: Not Included

EACH **VILLAIN** HAS A PARTICULAR **FOCUS** AND USES VARIOUS WAYS TO TRY TO REALIZE A **GOAL.**

THE VILLAINS

FEAR

I LIVE IN ANY DAMP, DARK, DANK, MUSTY, PLACE WITH ENOUGH ROOM FOR A GRATUITOUS DANCE NUMBER.

DOUBT

MY CHARACTERS DISPLAY THE FACT THAT THE DEVIL ALWAYS LOSES AND THE LORD ALWAYS WINS. EACH CHARACTER CREATES A PROBLEM—LIKE DOUBT, SADNESS, FEAR, PRIDE, OR ANGER—JUST LIKE ANY STRUGGLE WE, AS CHRISTIANS, FACE EVERY DAY.

—BRIAN LEMMONS

FURY

PRIDE

MISERY

BRIAN LEMMONS

Playing the role of the bad guy, Brian Lemmons joined the Bibleman team full-time in 1996. Brian says, "I didn't choose to be the villain, but Bibleman's job was already taken. Plus, the bad guy always gets the funniest lines."

So far, Brian has played Shadow of Doubt, Dr. Fear, Master of Misery, El Furioso, and Prince of Pride, both on stage and in video episodes. Since Bibleman defeats the villain each season—and in each video—a new bad guy must be developed for every new LIVE show and taped episode.

"Bibleman always defeats the bad guy," explains Brian. "And that makes my characters miserable and later ends their roles. So it's Bibleman's fault that I have to make a new costume every year. Do you know how long that takes me with a needle and thread?"

On the Bibleman LIVE tour, people often ask Brian why he is so evil and mean. He tells them, "If we don't show you kids the enemy, then you won't know how to defeat him!"

ONLY **BIBLEMAN** KNOWS WHO I REALLY AM...

I DON'T EVEN **KNOW** WHO I AM BECAUSE I KEEP **CHANGING** AND TRYING NEW THINGS THAT **NEVER WORK.**

FOR A GUY WHO KEEPS REINVENTING HIMSELF, YOU SURE DON'T FIGHT ANY **BETTER!**

SHADOW OF DOUBT

CONFIDENTIAL

U.N.I.C.E.L. REPORT

Name: Luxor Spawndroth

Code Name: Shadow of Doubt

Nickname: Shadow

Occupation: Satan's Minion

Sidekick: Ludicrous

Tools: Doubt Toxins

Tactics: The Shadow of Doubt uses his doubt toxins to persuade his victims to doubt their faith in their friends, family, and even in Christ.

Episode: Defeating the Shadow of Doubt

WHO HE IS:

SHADOW OF DOUBT TRIES TO GET CHRISTIANS TO DOUBT THEIR FAITH IN CHRIST WHILE **BIBLEMAN** USES **FAITH** TO DEFEAT DOUBT.

MASTER OF MISERY

LOOK, IT'S THE GRAPE IN A CAPE!

AS LONG AS THERE ARE GUYS LIKE YOU AROUND, THERE WILL ALWAYS BE GUYS DRESSED IN PURPLE SPANDEX LIKE ME.

CONFIDENTIAL
U.N.I.C.E. REPORT

NAME: Luxor Spawndroth

CODE NAME: Master of Misery

NICKNAME: Misery

OCCUPATION: Satan's Minion

SIDEKICKS: Ludicrous, L.U.C.I. (Link to Underhanded Computer Influences)

TOOLS: Anti-Joy Transmidifier, Endoplasmic Distortionary Syzmo-Ray

TACTICS: Misery uses his Endoplasmic Distortionary Syzmo-Ray to send a shock wave of depression or sadness to his victims.

EPISODE: The Incredible Force of Joy

WHO HE IS:

THE **MASTER OF MISERY** WANTS TO STEAL THE JOY FROM BELIEVERS AND MAKE THEM MISERABLE, WHILE **BIBLEMAN** USES THE JOY OF THE LORD AS HIS STRENGTH TO OVERCOME MISERY.

DR. FEAR

U.N.I.C.E. REPORT

Name:	Luxor Spawndroth
Code Name:	Dr. Fear
Occupation:	Satan's Minion
Sidekicks:	L.U.C.I..D.I.R.T. (Demons Inventing Rotten Tricks)
Tools:	Ether-Spectral Remote Control Device with Panic Button, Ultra-Pulse Vision Enhancing Lower Mandible
Tactics:	Digitizes interkinetic energy and transmits it as neural plutonic magnetic micro impulses which magnify the victim's inherent phobic reactions such as the fear of insect!
Episode:	The Fiendish Works of Dr. Fear

WHO HE IS:

DR. FEAR TRIES TO USE FEAR TO MAKE BELIEVERS TURN FROM CHRIST AND THEIR RESPONSIBILITIES AS CHRISTIANS, BUT **BIBLEMAN** RELIES ON THE SPIRIT OF BOLDNESS AND **COURAGE** TO DEFEAT FEAR.

PRINCE
OF PRIDE

WHO HE IS:

THE **PRINCE OF PRIDE** USES PRIDE TO TURN BELIEVERS AWAY FROM CHRISTIAN ATTITUDES, WHILE **BIBLEMAN** USES **HUMILITY** TO CONQUER PRIDE.

CONFIDENTIAL

U.N.I.C.E. REPORT

Name: Luxor Spawnroth

Code Name: Prince of Pride

Nickname: Pride, Prince (or the villain formally known as El Furioso)

Occupation: Satan's Minion

Sidekicks: Ludicrous, L.U.C.I

Tools: Shoulder Mounted Egoplasmic Adoration Ray

Tactics: Pride uses his shoulder-mounted ray to shoot the heads of his victims. The ray causes victims' heads to swell, resulting in self-centeredness. Victims think they are "better" or "above" others.

Episode: Shattering the Prince of Pride

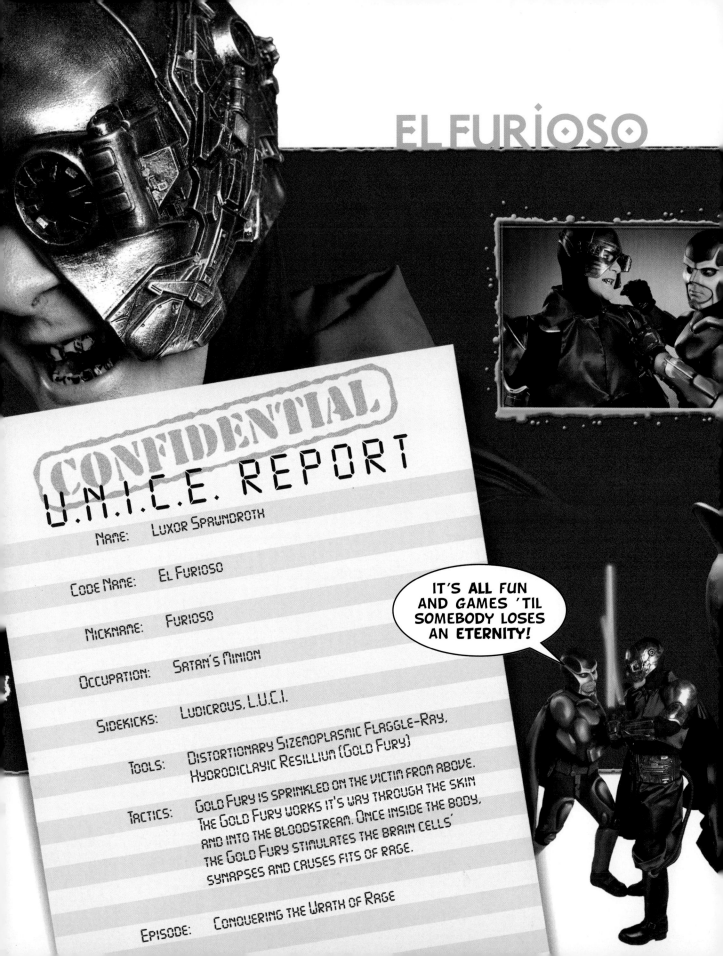

EL FURIOSO

CONFIDENTIAL
U.N.I.C.E. REPORT

NAME: Luxor Spawndroth

CODE NAME: El Furioso

NICKNAME: Furioso

OCCUPATION: Satan's Minion

SIDEKICKS: Ludicrous, L.U.C.I.

TOOLS: Distortionary Sizemoplasmic Flaggle-Ray, Hydrodiclayic Resillium (Gold Fury)

TACTICS: Gold Fury is sprinkled on the victim from above. The Gold Fury works it's way through the skin and into the bloodstream. Once inside the body, the Gold Fury stimulates the brain cells' synapses and causes fits of rage.

EPISODE: Conquering the Wrath of Rage

IT'S ALL FUN AND GAMES 'TIL SOMEBODY LOSES AN ETERNITY!

"THE **BIBLEMAN ADVENTURE**
IS ONE OF THE BEST I HAVE
EVER SEEN ... FAST-PACED,
EXCITING, AND RIVETING."

—JIM MULLEN,
*Crusade Director for the Billy Graham
Evangelical Association*

WHAT THE LIVE SHOW USED TO BE...
AND WHAT IT IS NOW!

Since I started with the Bibleman LIVE tour at the beginning, I've watched it emerge as a bookstore event with no music and no audience! We would only have ten kids show up—and we just had a boom box or tape deck. Now we have a full stage presentation with a ton of special effects, and we see hundreds of thousands of kids each year. It's amazing and humbling to see how God is using this ministry.

—BRIAN LEMMONS

THE BIBLEMAN
ADVENTURE LIVE

HOW THE LIVE SHOW COMES ABOUT:

The LIVE show takes months of preparation. We start with a theme or an idea that we believe God really wants us to talk about. Then we start brainstorming at least a year before the tour. We take time to think and pray about the ideas that we've brainstormed.

Once we decide on a theme, we choose Scripture that will best describe the tour. Then we sit and write ideas in the order that we think they will happen on the stage. We create an outline and then fill in the dialogue.

We'll write down new ideas and new dialogue. Once that's set, we will think about the stage, the props, and cool pyrotechnics we will use. Meanwhile, our booking coordinator is booking shows.

We start by designing the costumes, sketching designs for the stage, and working on the script. Then we schedule a two-week audio session to record all of the audio, the voices, and the music. We take two more weeks to edit the video and the digital graphics for the big screens.

During all of this, we are designing T-shirts, hats, posters, and having all of those things made. We hire the road crew, then we buy all of the lights, pyro, and stage equipment. And we have to do maintenance on the truck and the trailer.

Finally, we have to figure out how we will fit all of our stuff into the truck and trailer and travel across the country with it. Then, we go out on the road and see if it all works together . . . and we pray a lot!!!!

> When we're out on the road, I will take a bite of everything that is on my plate, and then I'll continue to talk while the food is falling out of my mouth onto the table. It grosses the other guys out.
>
> **WiLLiE**

ON THE ROAD

> I love traveling, seeing different cities, and meeting so many great people across the country. I love being able to perform and minister at the same time. There is nothing else I would want to do. This is definitely an answered prayer.
>
> **BRADY**

> On the road, I dress so bad that I embarrass the road crew. I wear worn out high-top tennis shoes, red hunting socks, and shorts into restaurants. Finally, a crew member called my wife and asked her to make me dress better!
>
> **WiLLiE**

> The longest time we went without sleep is 43 hours straight! Each year we cover enough miles to circle the globe more than twice. We see over 200,000 people every year. Being on the road is fun, exciting, scary, tiring, hard, satisfying, and lonely. It's fun to meet people across the country and then see them year after year. It's like having family across the country.
>
> **WiLLiE**

> One of the funniest things I remember after a show is when a kid asked me what I wear underneath my suit. Thinking fast, I told him I had on my "Biblebriefs." And that's what they've been called to this day!
>
> **WILLIE**

WILD AND CRAZY CHRISTIANS IN A TRUCK:

We started with a Ryder truck with four people in the cab, then we upgraded to a family van with a trailer, then to a converted Ryder van, and finally this year, we got a tour bus! It's been long, and sometimes rough, but people have finally been able to see the vision and get the message. Each year we reach more kids. Each year the message gets stronger. —**BRIAN**

I can tell you that being stuffed in a bus with a bunch of Christian guys is a wild and crazy experience! —**BRADY**

We all travel together in the vehicle. There are five of us: me, Brady, Brian, our light guy, and the road manager. We eat, sleep, and ride within fifteen inches of each other. We each have our own bunk with a little basket for our belongings. Not too much space. It's like living in a small bedroom with your whole family! This is the second year that we have had a driver. For three years, we did all of the driving ourselves. It is really nice (and a lot safer) to have a driver. He has a completely different schedule than we do. He sleeps all day and drives all night. —**WILLIE**

WHERE ELSE DO YOU KEEP YOUR STUFF?

I keep my dirty socks in Brian's bunk! —**WILLIE**

WHAT DO YOU DO WHEN YOU'RE ON THE ROAD?

We watch videos: we pick one and watch it over and over again. We like getting movies that look like they will be really stupid. Then we walk around for about a month acting like the characters. —**WILLIE**

DO YOU ALWAYS SLEEP IN THE TRUCK?

We sleep about anywhere we can, including under pews in churches, and on pews in churches. —**WILLIE**

THE BIBLEMAN

ADVENTURE LIVE ON STAGE...

My goal is to be very honest with the audience. I want to make sure that the show points them to Jesus FIRST! I want them to know that I am just a man. It is a relationship with Jesus that makes my life special. I'm there to get the audience excited, to entertain them, to encourage them, to make them laugh and think. I am there for parents to relate to because I am a parent. I am there to help kids see the reality of Jesus Christ.
—**WILLIE**

When I was a kid, we didn't have cool, high-tech Christian entertainment. I was stuck with the stuff on TV. Now I have a chance to change that for kids today and give them a good high quality show in a Christian format. I am all over that. —**BRIAN**

God tells us to have the faith of a child. I love to see kids' innocence when we meet them on tour—especially during the salvation message at the end of the program when they come forward to begin their relationship with Christ. God is really using this ministry—I'm humbled to be a part of it. —**BRADY**

There's not a whole lot out there like this—cutting edge, up-to-date stuff with the cool gadgets, special effects, and pyrotechnics—that also includes a positive Christian message. It is really important to me that we are reaching thousands of kids each year with the Gospel message! —**BRIAN**

SETTING UP THE LIVE SHOW:

When we get to the church, we have to load in all of the set and reconstruct it. Then we have just enough time to grab something to eat and change into costume. After the show, we meet with all of the kids, then we have to tear down the set and load it back into our truck. We usually get done about one or two in the morning, and then we go get some dinner. We get some sleep on the road or at the church, and then we're up in the morning, heading out to the next location! It's a crazy schedule! —WILLIE

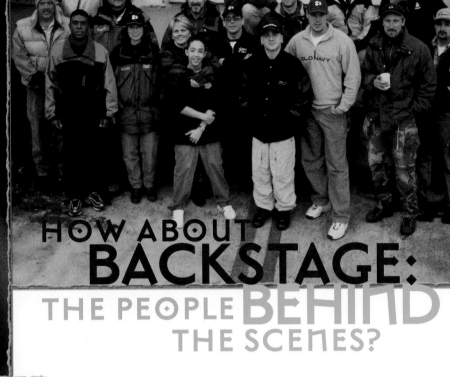

HOW ABOUT BACKSTAGE:
THE PEOPLE BEHIND THE SCENES?

Q What's it like backstage? Do you have techies handling everything, or does the church provide them? Who are the people behind you that we can't see? How do they fit in? Tell us about the people who run sound, lights, pyrotechnics, etc.?

A We do it all! It actually is pretty funny. When there are one or two of us on stage, the other is back behind the set pushing buttons for pyro, then we run out and do our line, then run back and push another button—all throughout the show.

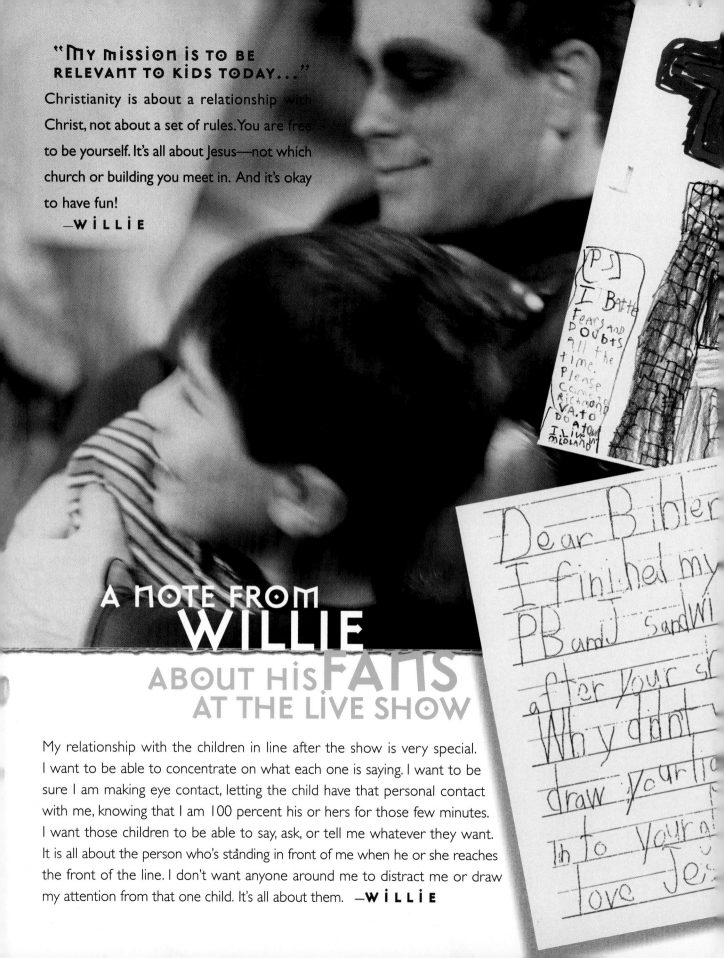

"MY MISSION IS TO BE RELEVANT TO KIDS TODAY..."

Christianity is about a relationship with Christ, not about a set of rules. You are free to be yourself. It's all about Jesus—not which church or building you meet in. And it's okay to have fun!

—WiLLiE

A NOTE FROM WILLIE
ABOUT HIS FANS
AT THE LIVE SHOW

My relationship with the children in line after the show is very special. I want to be able to concentrate on what each one is saying. I want to be sure I am making eye contact, letting the child have that personal contact with me, knowing that I am 100 percent his or hers for those few minutes. I want those children to be able to say, ask, or tell me whatever they want. It is all about the person who's standing in front of me when he or she reaches the front of the line. I don't want anyone around me to distract me or draw my attention from that one child. It's all about them. **—WiLLiE**

THANK YOU LOCK...

LOCKheed vega

BY Pete.

Bibleman

Perry

super

Perry H. Age 5

FLOYD COUNTY, GEORGIA
POLICE DEPARTMENT

JIM FREE
CHIEF

BILL SHIFLETT
ASSISTANT CHIEF

TOMMY SHIFLETT
...ESTIGATOR

...FREEMAN
...ER OF
...ISION

...NER
...TRAINING
L AFFAIRS

July 2, 1999

Mr. Donnie Slade
The Church at Northside
3006 Martha Berry Highway
Rome, Georgia 30165

Dear Donnie:

I wanted to let you know how disgusted I was with the Bibleman Show.
When I suggested to Ivanette that it might be a good program for our two
grand children I envisioned that she would be the one to bring them.
Ivanette had a different idea and I had to come along with her. When we
arrived at the forum I was not a happy camper. The music was too loud,
the room was filled with smoke and the show was late getting started. My
back was hurting and I decided to get everyone a Coke. I thought that was
a pretty simple order but when I got back to my seat I soon discovered that
the girl had given me four Dr. Peppers. Finally the show was over and I
think my prayer was thank God surely you wouldn't want me to endure
anymore of this silly show. Then Bibleman gave the invitation and I sensed
that my oldest grand daughter Abbi was raising her hand. I knew that her
uncle Jason and her mom had been talking to her about salvation and that
recently she had been asking questions. Ivanette carried her down and with
the help of one of the staff Abbie accepted Christ. I soon forgot about my
back, the loud music and the Dr. Pepper and began to thank God for you,
Bibleman and all the staff of Northside for making this show possible.
The message God delivered through this ministry was just what this
precious little girl needed to lead her to accept Jesus Christ as her savior.

Thank you for your dedication to the children of Rome and Floyd County
and to the Bibleman ministry for turning a pretty dull evening into one of
the best moments of my life.

Sincerely,

Free

FIVE GOVERNMENT PLAZA POST OFFICE BOX 946 ROME, GEORGIA 30161-2802
PHONE (706) 235-7766 FAX (706) 291-5224

Helen Hunt and Eric Olson starred with Willie Aames in *Swiss Family Robinson*, an ABC family series that aired on Saturdays.

The successful ABC series *Eight Is Enough* featured Willie as Tommy Bradford from 1974-1980.

Willie's band, Paradise, found popularity among teens, but the band never released an album.

WILLIE AAMES: THE MAN BEHIND THE MASK

HiS FiRST **BiG** SERiES HiT

Eight is Enough ran on ABC from 1974-1980. It was the story of a man with eight kids. I played the middle son, Tommy, who played in a rock-and-roll band. It was a wholesome family comedy/drama, very much like *Seventh Heaven* is today, only cornier. It was the #1 show in the country for several years. I played so much music on the program that I eventually ended up writing music for the show.

FUNNY STUFF

We'd pick one actor, and then the rest of the entire crew would secretly put rocks into the chosen actor's duffel bag during shooting. So their bag would gradually get heavier and heavier throughout the day's shooting.

HOW DiD YOU BREAK iNTO SHOW BUSiNESS?

When I was eight years old, a teacher's boyfriend saw me in some school plays. He thought I had some talent, and he introduced me to my first agent. My very first job was a Phillips 66 commercial. At the time, if you bought an entire tank of gas, they would give you a free set of glasses. So, I played a boy selling lemonade (with my Phillips 66 glasses) to an old prospector, who liked my lemonade so much that he gave me an entire bag of gold! The funny thing was, I did this entire commercial with my zipper unzipped. So we had to do the whole commercial all over again!

ANOTHER HIT FOLLOWS WITH
CHARLES IN CHARGE...

Charles in Charge aired from 1983 through 1990. It was the story of a live-in nanny (played by Scott Baio) working his way through college. It was very similar to *Who's the Boss.* I played Scott's best friend.

FUNNY STUFF

I used to eat a whole RAW onion before close-up scenes with Scott Baio. I wanted to see if I could get him to gag because my breath was so bad!

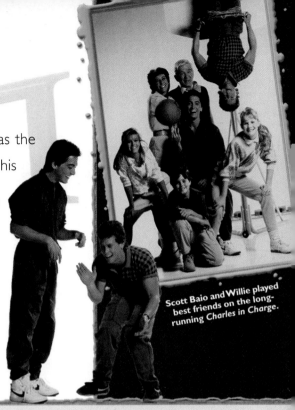

Scott Baio and Willie played best friends on the long-running *Charles in Charge.*

DID EARLY ACTING SUCCESS BOTHER YOU AS A CHILD?

I started so young, that lifestyle (school on set, catered food, etc.) was really all I knew. I guess if I had to say one thing that bothered me the most was the fact that I knew I wasn't as big of a deal as everyone thought I was. The other thing that really bothered me was that I had more "stuff" than everyone else. I didn't and still don't like seeing people in need.

WHO WERE YOUR HEROES WHEN YOU WERE A CHILD?

When I was a child, my own favorite heroes were Errol Flynn, Robin Hood, Woody Woodpecker, and Mike Nelson. I loved adventure and all of these characters were adventure heroes. As a kid, I always looked for adventurous games, ideas, and things to do. When I was older, I became a scuba diver because of Mike Nelson, an actor on *Sea Hunt.*

WHAT DID YOU LIKE BEST ABOUT BEING A FAMOUS KID?

I loved having the ability to buy my family presents and help other people that were in need.

WHAT'S ONE OF YOUR FAVORITE CHILDHOOD MEMORIES?

My family had a real love for the Mexican people, and every summer, we drove down to Mexico. We stayed in a tent and distributed food and supplies to Mexican citizens who were in need.

THE WORST IDEA
HE'D EVER HEARD!

HOW DID YOU DECIDE TO BECOME BIBLEMAN?

After I left Los Angeles, I moved to Kansas City where I thought to produce fishing shows and relax. Little did I know that God had something else in store. After living in Kansas for several years, I received a phone call from some men in Dallas, Texas. They said that they knew about my Hollywood career and that they had my next "big" career move all planned out.

So I flew to Texas and met with them. During lunch they looked me right in the face and said "Are you ready? We think you need to become Bibleman!"

I about fell out of my chair. "That's the worst idea I have ever heard in my life," I told them. "What in the world is a Bibleman? And what does he do?"

Amazingly, five years, seven videos, four US tours, and hundreds of thousands of kids later, I am truly blessed to be "the worst idea" I had ever heard.

WHY LIVE PERFORMANCE ART FOR CHRIST?

We are pioneers. This is new to the entertainment industry. I love that we are able to break the "industry" rules, yet be loyal to Christ. We are overtly Christian and evangelical, yet we can still compete with any secular production out there. We have plenty of room to grow and get better and get bigger. We have a lot to prove, and we get the chance to do it. —WILLIE